RICHARD SCARRY'S
Great Big Schoolhouse
Readers

Ice Cream
for Breakfast

Illustrated by Huck Scarry
Written by Erica Farber

STERLING

New York / London
www.sterlingpublishing.com/kids

RING! RING!

"Hello," said Huckle.

"Do you know what today is?"
asked Bridget.
"It's backward
day!"

2

Huckle walked backward up the stairs.

He didn't see Sally. Oops!

Huckle put on his
shirt backward.

He put on his pants backward.

He put on his hat backward.
Lowly did, too.

Knock-knock! It was Bridget.
She was just in time for dinner.
Dinner is always before breakfast
on backward day.

First, they ate ice cream.

Then they ate pizza.

Yum! Yum!

They walked to the bus stop backward.

They got on the bus backward.

But the bus driver made
them sit forward.
Thank you, bus driver!

Miss Honey asked them to write
their names backward.

E-L-K-C-U-H is Huckle spelled
backward.

Lowly thought hard about
how to write his name backward.
He broke the chalk!

At recess, Arthur went backward down the slide. "Oops!" he said.

"Spoo!" said Molly.
"That's *oops* spelled backward!"

Skip and Frances played
basketball backward.

Huckle and Lowly played
soccer backward.

Watch out! LAOG!

Then they all played
hide-and-seek backward.
"You found us. Now we'll go hide,"
said Bridget to Huckle.

"Three, two, one—ready
or not, here I come!" said Huckle.
"You mean one, two, three!"
said Bridget.

Then it was time for the class play.

It was the story of Cinderella.

The ending came first.

Here's how it went:

Cinderella married the prince.

Then she lost her slipper.

The clock struck midnight.

The fairy godmother turned the

pumpkin into a coach.

She turned two mice into footmen.

The evil stepmother handed
Cinderella a broom and told her
to clean.

The beginning was last.
Miss Honey clapped and clapped.

Everyone bowed backward!

Backward day was almost over.

Huckle had breakfast for dinner.

He had cereal and orange juice.

Then he put
on his pajamas
backward.

He brushed
his teeth
backward.

The toothpaste got on
his nose. CHOO-AH!

RING! RING!

"Hello," said Huckle.

"Do you know what tomorrow is?"
asked Bridget.

"Upside-down day! I'm doing a
headstand right now."

Huckle did a headstand, too.
He was so tired from going
backward all day.

He fell asleep upside down!

STERLING and the distinctive Sterling logo are registered trademarks of
Sterling Publishing Co., Inc.

Library of Congress Cataloging-in-Publication Data Available

Lot #: 10 9 8 7 6 5 4 3 2
09/11
Published by Sterling Publishing Co., Inc.
387 Park Avenue South, New York, NY 10016

In association with JB Publishing, Inc.
121 West 27th Street, Suite 902, New York, NY 10001

Text © 2011 JB Publishing, Inc.
Illustrations © 2011 Richard Scarry Corporation
All characters are the property of the Richard Scarry Corporation.

Distributed in Canada by Sterling Publishing
c/o Canadian Manda Group, 165 Dufferin Street
Toronto, Ontario, Canada M6K 3H6
Distributed in the United Kingdom by GMC Distribution Services
Castle Place, 166 High Street, Lewes, East Sussex, England BN7 1XU
Distributed in Australia by Capricorn Link (Australia) Pty. Ltd.
P.O. Box 704, Windsor, NSW 2756, Australia

produced by   JR Sansevere

Printed in China
All rights reserved

Sterling ISBN: 978-1-4027-8449-1 (hardcover)
              978-1-4027-7320-4 (paperback)

For information about custom editions, special sales, premium and
corporate purchases, please contact Sterling Special Sales
Department at 800-805-5489 or specialsales@sterlingpublishing.com.